For Nicola, Eliza,
Jack and Tom
A.M.

For Miles, with love
J.M.

This edition published in 2002.

Text copyright © 1995 by Anne Mangan.

Illustrations copyright © 1995 by Joanne Moss.

Published by Troll Communications L.L.C.

Reprinted by arrangement with Little Tiger Press,
an imprint of Magi Publications, London.

ISBN 0-8167-7589-3

Printed in the United States of America.

10 9 8 7 6 5 4 3 2 1

Little Teddy Left Behind

by Anne Mangan
Pictures by Joanne Moss

Troll

Little Teddy woke up and sneezed loudly.

Nobody heard him because there was no one there. Nicole and Jack had moved to a new house.

"I'm all alone," said Teddy. "They've left me behind. They never were very good at packing." It was so dusty that he sneezed again. "Achoo!"

It grew dark, and at last Teddy went to sleep again.

The next morning the cleaning lady's dog spotted him and picked him up.

"What do you have there?" asked the lady, and when she saw how grubby Teddy was, she grabbed him with her big hands . . .

. . . and popped him into the washing machine!

"Oh, help!" cried Little Teddy, but she didn't hear his tiny squeak.

It was terrible in the washing machine. Teddy whirled around and around until he was quite dizzy. He growled his very loudest growl, but nobody came to rescue him. At last he was spun dry, and the machine stopped. Teddy lay there among all the damp clothes, wondering what would happen next.

The cleaning lady opened the machine door and
took him out. "You're not quite dry yet," she said.

"I am so!" growled Little Teddy, but she didn't
seem to hear. In a moment she'd pinned him upside
down on the clothesline. "I'd rather be dirty and right
side up!" he cried.

It was a windy day, and Teddy swung back and forth on the clothesline. It was exciting in a way, like flying in space.

All at once the line broke, and Teddy fell down, down, down. "It's a good thing bears have so much fluff," he thought as he landed in the grass. Butterflies flew around him and bees buzzed over his head. Little Teddy liked the bright, cheerful butterflies, but he was afraid of the bees.

"You scare me," he squeaked, even though they were too busy to hear him.

Suddenly Teddy felt hot breath in his ear.

"Oh no!" he cried. "It's that dog again!"

The dog seized Little Teddy in his big teeth and pushed through a very prickly hedge into the next garden.

"Oh, my poor fur!" gasped Teddy.

A lady looked up as the dog rushed onto her lawn. "Ugh, you've got a rat in your mouth!" she screamed, throwing her garden glove at them.

"I'm no rat!" growled Teddy.

The dog ran out through the garden gate into the woods.

"I wish he'd drop me," thought poor Teddy. Finally, the dog spotted a rabbit and ran off, leaving Teddy behind.

Teddy lay very still, hoping the dog wouldn't come back. It was quiet in the woods—but not for long. A boy and a girl came rushing toward him.

"Hey, a little teddy!" cried the boy, picking him up.

"Catch!" he shouted, and poor
Teddy was tossed from one to the other until
he felt quite sick. Jack and Nicole had never played
with him like this.

At last the children grew tired of their game, and
the girl flung Little Teddy high into the air.

Up, up, up he sailed, right into the branches of a
tall tree. No sooner had he landed than he heard an
angry chattering noise.

"Trying to steal my nuts, are you?"

Teddy looked down from his perch. On the next branch a squirrel was glaring at him. Teddy tried to explain about the boy and girl and their awful game of catch, but the squirrel didn't seem to hear. "This is my tree!" he said, giving Teddy a sudden push. The little bear fell down, down, down . . .

. . . and landed on a wooden floor.

He was still getting his breath back and
wondering how Jack and Nicole would ever
find him, when he heard children's voices.
He tried his growl and he tried his squeak,
but they were too small for anyone to hear him.

The floor was as dusty as the empty room
he had left behind. Once again Little Teddy
began to sneeze and sneeze. The sneezes were
louder than the growls and squeaks, and soon the
voices came nearer . . .

"Look, there's a ladder!"

"It's a tree house!"

Two faces were peering at him—two faces he knew very well!

"It's Little Teddy!" cried Jack. "How did he get in our new yard? I thought he was still packed up."

"I don't know," said Nicole, giving Teddy a hug. "Maybe he's been exploring his new home. What a wonderful tree house he's found!"

"Let's call it the Teddy House," said Jack.

His very own house! Little Teddy liked the idea.

A few days later, Nicole and Jack had
a housewarming party for all their friends.
And each friend brought a teddy bear, so
that Little Teddy could have his *own* party
in his new home in the big tree.